Shapeshifters Productions
Raritan, NJ
©2020

To all the people who have supported me in pursuing art, as well as all the essential workers, families, healthcare workers, and educators who have been working hard through COVID-19. H.M.

To my students and friends who miss the people they love, and to all the people I miss. E.B.

Corona-Alona

Written by
Emily Bengels

Illustrated by
Hannah Mills

Shapeshifters Productions, Raritan, NJ
©2020

Normally, the house woke up in the morning just in time to say goodbye to the children who ran off to school and the parents who ran off to work.

It would watch as they went away, and then spend the day alone.

Well, not exactly alone...
There was a naughty dog who lived
there, and two cuddly cats.

But houses like people, so the house felt alone. She waited each day, patiently, for her people to come home.

Then one day, her people came home and stayed.

But something was different about the family when they stayed home all the time.

Maybe it was the way everyone washed their hands more than ever before. They even sang the whole alphabet each time!

Maybe it was the way the grownups scrubbed down everything again and again and again.

They even sprayed the grocery bags and the mail before bringing anything into the house!

Maybe it was the way laughing voices came to the house each night on the computer. Later, children's voices would come to the computer and practice reading to one another, pretending the computer was school. The house found it all to be very confusing.

The house liked having everybody home,
especially when they all read together on the couch...

...and when they had fun cooking together.

The house didn't feel so alone anymore, even if it was a confusing time.

She liked watching her people take time to build towers together, solve puzzles together, and create music together.

She wasn't so alone anymore.

Above all, the house loved the mornings.

Everyone got up when they wanted to. There was no rush to get anywhere. There was no rush to get dressed, or to leave for work. The family just didn't leave the house. And so the house wasn't alone anymore.

However, the house knew her people had problems,
so she started listening to see how she could help.

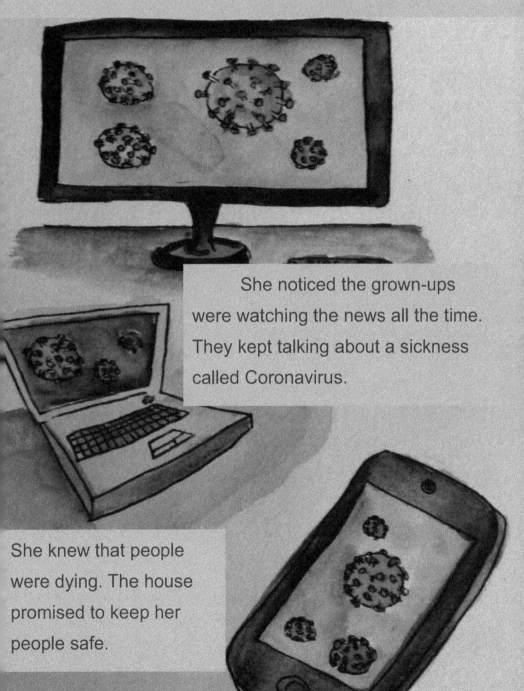

She noticed the grown-ups
were watching the news all the time.
They kept talking about a sickness
called Coronavirus.

She knew that people
were dying. The house
promised to keep her
people safe.

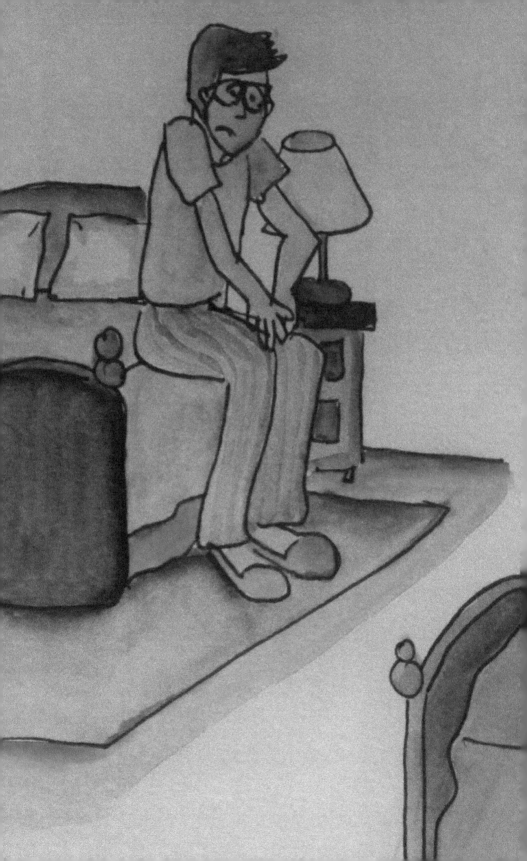

At night, the house
heard the grown-ups
talking in whispers.

She saw everyone
cry sometimes.

She tried to comfort
the children when
they had nightmares.

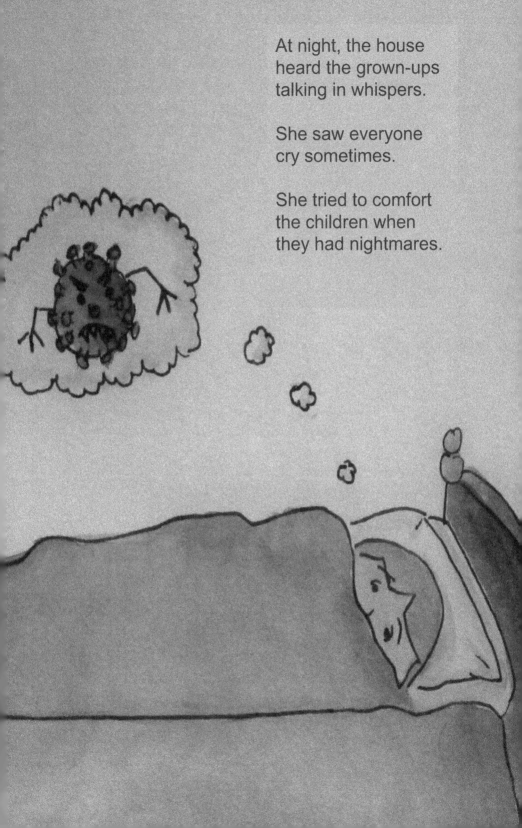

Luckily, it was spring. The house opened her windows wide and let the gentle breeze dance inside. She welcomed in the smell of new flowers.

She hoped this would cheer up her people.

At first, the family took long walks. They even went to parks with the naughty puppy, and the children played in playgrounds. But then the news-people said the parks would close. Now, children couldn't play in playgrounds anymore.

The worst was when the little girl started crying. "My birthday is canceled because of the virus," she said.

The house didn't know how to comfort her.

"I'm so lonely! This is the **corona-alona** virus," the little girl wept to her mother.

The house liked to help, but she didn't know how to talk. Instead, she found all sorts of treasures hidden away in cupboards and closets and little drawers.

She found a craft box with paints. She found a collection of big white stones. She found big poster paper.

The house creaked a bit near where the treasures were hidden. Before long, the family found the treasures too!

The next day, the family started making crafts together. They decorated the stones with happy messages.

They made posters with big thank you signs.

Then, they went for a walk with the naughty dog.

They left the happiness stones near neighbors' houses. They put the "Thank you!" Posters up on the fences of doctors' offices and outside of grocery stores and pharmacies. The little girl liked helping so much that she forgot she was lonely!

"I'm happy," said the little girl, "I'm happy we can help.

But when will we see Grandma and Grandpa? I want to hug them!"

"We can't see them right now, but let's draw them pictures and send them cards." And so they did.

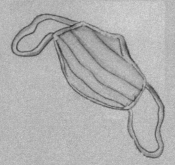

It would be a long time before life could go back to normal. It would be a new normal. People would have to wear masks. People would lose jobs. Some people would get sick .

But the family would stick together. They would read and cook and make artwork, they would call their friends and family from afar, and no matter what they did, the house would take care of them.

Afterwards, the family would remember to read together and eat together and even do crafts together more than before.

They would call their grandparents and make pictures for people they missed.

Afterwards, when the kids went back to school and the grown-ups went back to work, the house wouldn't be alone as much anymore, because the family wanted together-time more.

And, when the little girl had her next birthday, she would tell everyone that it wasn't really the "Corona-Alona" virus.

In fact, it was the **Corona-let's-stick-together** virus.

She would blow out the candles and wish for everyone to be happy and healthy and together. Then she'd go play outside with her friends.

The End…

and the beginning a new normal…

Together!

CPSIA information can be obtained
at www.ICGtesting.com
Printed in the USA
BVHW022044280720
584907BV00017B/535